A SECRET KEEPS

For Grampa John, Jaden, and Ethan
—M. W. C.

For Tiger, Nemo, Krack, Sootie, and their people
—H. S.

Text copyright © 2012 by Marsha Wilson Chall
Illustrations copyright © 2012 by Heather M. Solomon

Carolrhoda Books
A division of Lerner Publishing Group, Inc.
241 First Avenue North
Minneapolis, MN 55401 U.S.A.

Website address: www.lernerbooks.com

Main body text set in Atelier Sans 18/26.
Typeface provided by International Typeface Corp.

Library of Congress Cataloging-in-Publication Data

Chall, Marsha Wilson.
    A secret keeps / by Marsha Wilson Chall.
        p.   cm.
    Summary: Relates, in rhyming text, a child's trip from his urban home to his
grandparents' farm, where a secret surprise awaits at the end of a long weekend.
    ISBN: 978–0–7613–5593–9 (lib. bdg. : alk. paper)
    [1. Stories in rhyme. 2. Grandparents—Fiction. 3. Farm life—Fiction.
4. Domestic animals—Fiction. 5. Secrets—Fiction.] I. Title.
PZ8.3.C356Se 2012
[E]—dc23   2011021241

Manufactured in the United States of America
1 – PP – 12/31/11

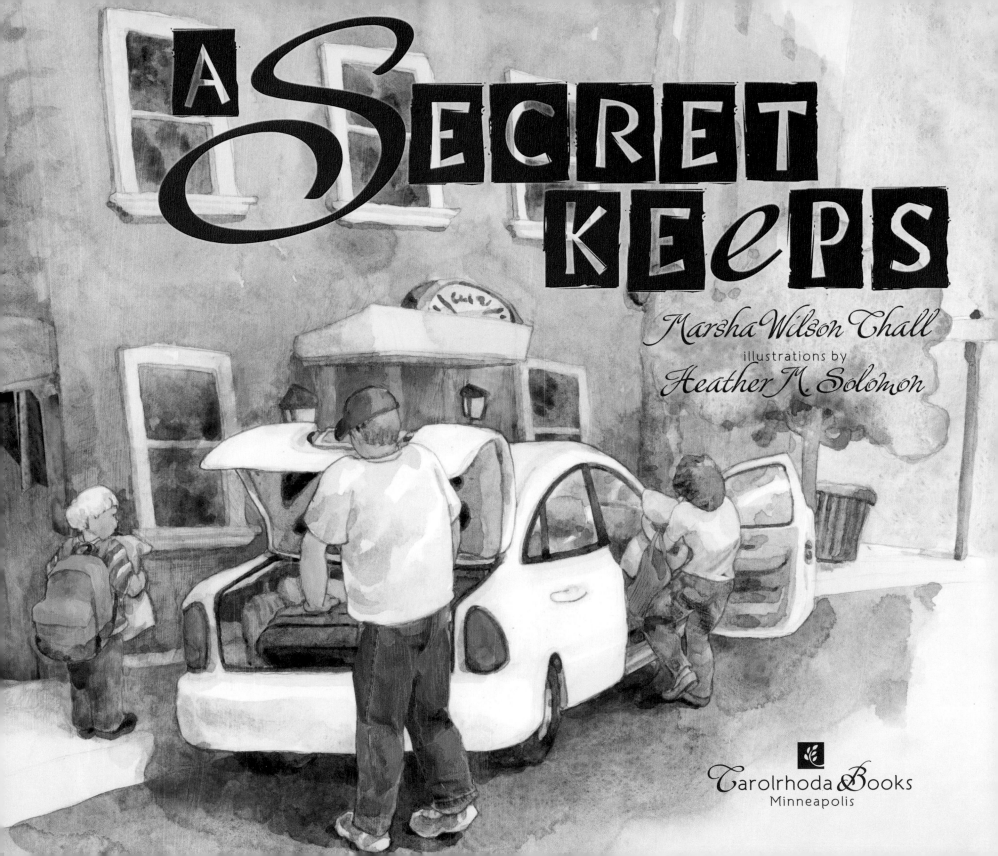

A Secret Keeps

Marsha Wilson Chall

illustrations by
Heather M. Solomon

Carolrhoda Books
Minneapolis

Past towers and trestles,
fences and fields,
the moon follows me to the farm.

Grampa said something's waiting for me,
and I can't wait to know what.

"No secrets, Grampa," I told him.
All he said was, "See you soon."

Mom says we'll get there faster
if I take a nap or two.
I'll be there in two sleeps
where A SECRET KEEPS.
Something's hiding under the moon.

Jillions of peeper frogs leap and peep
out behind the barn.
Grampa stokes a fire.
Flames flick against the sky.

He whittles sticks for roasting.
"Here, give this a try."
I spear two marshmallows,
then toast them till they're golden.
Mmmmm, just right—
warm, sweet, molten.

Night tucks in around us
and rustles in the dark.
"Grampa, where's the secret?"
"Finders, keepers," is all he says.
"Whoo-hoo," says owl.
Coyote yips.
Stars blink above the barn.
Little sky spies—
can they spot a secret?
Wish I had their eyes.

Cock-ee-doodlely-doo!
Old Rudy crows in the barnyard.
"Rise and shine," Gramma calls up the stairs.

Out to the henhouse we go.
"Gramma, do you know the secret?"
"A secret is for keeping," she says.
The chickens cluck, *That's true.*

Brown egg, white, green, and blue
as smooth as Gramma's china,
thin shells I can't peek through.
I listen for the secret,
but no doodlely or a doo.

In the barn, cats stretch and preen
on thrones of straw and hay.
Your Highnesses, what's the secret?
Please grant me just one clue.
Cali Cat stares. Gus licks his paws.
It's not a secret if you tell—
still I wish I knew.

Or is the secret up above
in the barn's great rafters,
where swallows in tuxedo tails
swoop through speckled air
with bits of this and tufts of that.
Is the secret hiding there?

Could it be in Grampa's cornfield?
It must have heard the secret—
you know it is all ears.

Something cuckles down a row.
Ring-neck pheasant flushes.
What secret does he know?

Round brown cow,
eating is your work.
Too busy to tell secrets,
chewing cud all day—

is something hiding in your stack
of sweet alfalfa hay?

We call the cows home after supper,
wash up for peach pie a la mode,
then share a game of checkers
and bedtime with Frog and Toad.

But I can't close my eyes just yet.
The moon is watching me.
If I see the moon and the moon sees me,
I wonder what else the moon can see.

It must be full of secrets
whispered in the night.
Show me, moon, what's hiding
in the shadows of your light.
It streaks a silver sliver,
a moonbeam tightrope on the floor.
Heel to toe, I cross it
and slip out the kitchen door.

Moonlight floods the farmyard.
My arms look almost blue.
Somewhere past the henhouse,
I think I hear, *mew.*

I creep toward the barn
floating in a milky sea,
then board the glowing galleon.
I'm a pirate with the key.

Where is the secret treasure?
A critter skitters in the hay.
The barn's black as crows at midnight.
I'll have to feel my way.

I find the ladder,
take a breath,
then climb up to the loft.
Shhhh, the pirate hushes.
Then something brushes,
something soft.

A moonbeam shines a haymow stage.
Gus and Cali lead the show.
It's midnight at the cat dance,
kittens pouncing high and low.

One curls around my ankle.
I scoop up the ball of fur.
Are you my secret, kitten?
She blinks and thrums a purr.

"Gramma, Grampa—can I keep her?
You know a secret is for keeping."

They kiss my head and tuck us in.
Shhhh—my Secret's sleeping.